This book belongs to

....

....

....

This edition published by Parragon Books Ltd in 2014
and distributed by

Parragon Inc.
440 Park Avenue South, 13th Floor
New York, NY 10016
www.parragon.com

ISBN 978-1-4723-4537-0

Printed in China

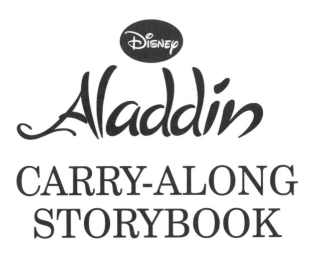

CARRY-ALONG
STORYBOOK

Bath · New York · Cologne · Melbourne · Delhi
Hong Kong · Shenzhen · Singapore · Amsterdam

Once upon a time, in the city of Agrabah, there lived an evil sorcerer named Jafar. He was the advisor to the Sultan of Agrabah.

Deep in the Arabian Desert, Jafar placed two halves of a magical beetle together. It glowed to life and flew across the desert. When it stopped, the sand rose up to form a huge head of a tiger revealing the entrance to the Cave of Wonders!

"At last—the Cave of Wonders!" said Jafar.
He ordered a thief named Gazeem to enter the cave to fetch a magic lamp.
"Remember, bring me the lamp," he told Gazeem. "Then the rest of the treasure is yours."

As Gazeem stepped into the cave, a mystical voice boomed: "Only one may enter here—the diamond in the rough!" Suddenly, the cave's entrance clamped shut, trapping Gazeem inside. The tiger's head quickly dissolved into the sand.

Iago, Jafar's parrot, asked: "What are we going to do now?"

"I must find this . . . diamond in the rough," declared Jafar.

   The next morning, in the marketplace of Agrabah,
a poor young man named Aladdin was on the run
because he had stolen a loaf of bread. The guards of
the Sultan were chasing him.
   "Stop, street rat!" they shouted. Aladdin and his pet
monkey, Abu, fled over rooftops and balconies, up
steps, and down alleyways.

Aladdin and Abu outwitted the guards and joyfully escaped with their lunch. The two friends had not eaten a decent meal in weeks!

But then Aladdin saw two hungry children being told off by a cruel prince. Aladdin rushed to the children's rescue and gave them his bread. He and Abu went home with empty bellies.

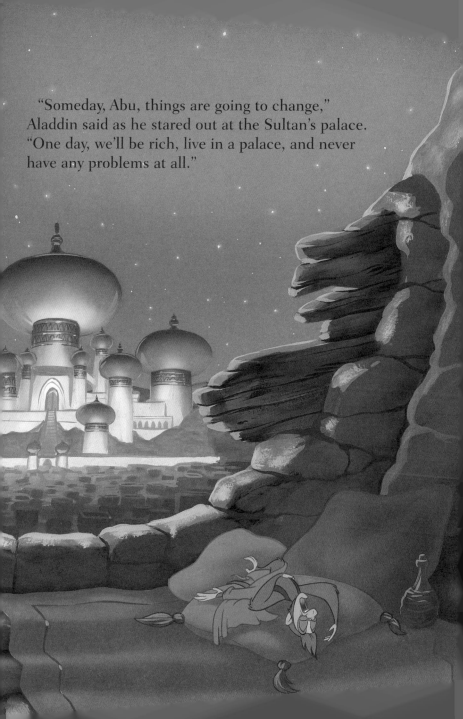

"Someday, Abu, things are going to change,"
Aladdin said as he stared out at the Sultan's palace.
"One day, we'll be rich, live in a palace, and never
have any problems at all."

Meanwhile, in the palace, Princess Jasmine
was very unhappy. Her father, the Sultan, wanted
to marry her off to a prince in three days!

"It's the law," he told Jasmine. "You are a
princess."

But the princess only wanted to marry for love.
"Maybe I don't want to be a princess anymore,"
she replied as she patted her tiger Rajah.
"I've never even been outside the palace walls."

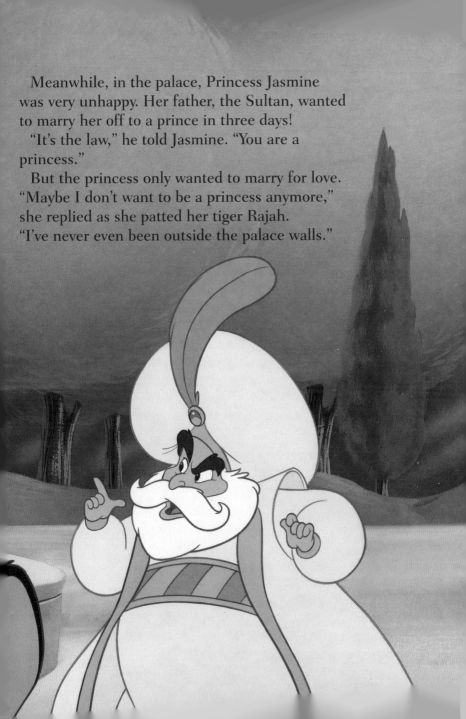

The Sultan was at his wits' end! He called upon Jafar for help.

"Jafar, my most trusted advisor, I am in desperate need of your wisdom," pleaded the Sultan. "Jasmine refuses to choose a husband."

"Perhaps I can devise a solution," said Jafar. "But I would require the use of the mystic blue diamond on your ring."

The Sultan did not want to give up his cherished ring, but Jafar used his snake staff to hypnotize him and took the ring!

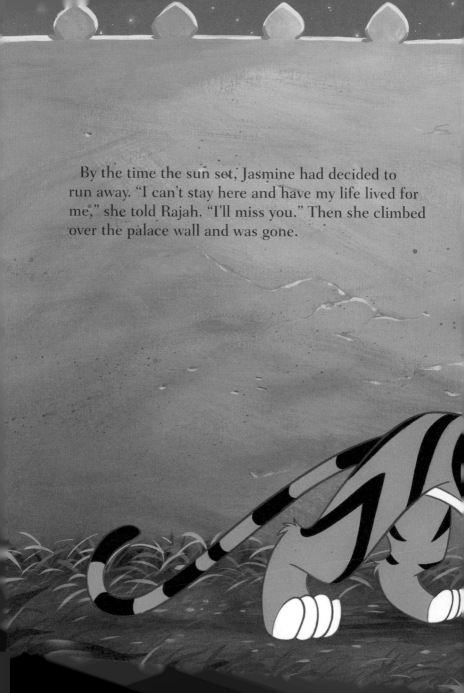

By the time the sun set, Jasmine had decided to run away. "I can't stay here and have my life lived for me," she told Rajah. "I'll miss you." Then she climbed over the palace wall and was gone.

Soon Jasmine found herself in a new world—
Agrabah's bustling marketplace. The beautiful
princess quickly caught the attention of Aladdin,
and he began to watch her.

Seeing a young, hungry child, Jasmine picked an apple from a fruit stand and gave it to him. The princess didn't realize she would have to pay.

"You'd better be able to pay for that!" bellowed the huge fruit seller.

"I don't have any money!" cried Jasmine.

"Thief!" shouted the vendor.

Just then, Aladdin appeared and defended Jasmine. Quickly, he led her away.

"So, where are you from?" Aladdin asked, leading
Jasmine to his rooftop home.

"I ran away," Jasmine answered with a sigh.
"My father is forcing me to get married."

"That's awful," Aladdin said.

Meanwhile, at his secret chamber in the palace, Jafar used the Sultan's ring to find out who would be able to enter the Cave of Wonders.

"Show me the diamond in the rough," he commanded the magical hourglass. An image of Aladdin appeared! Jafar quickly ordered the Sultan's guards to find Aladdin and bring him to the palace.

The palace guards found Aladdin's home and captured the street rat.

Jasmine threw off her scarf. "Unhand him, by order of the princess," she demanded. The captain, shocked to see the princess, said: "I would, Princess, but my orders come from Jafar." Jasmine immediately hurried back to the palace to confront Jafar.

Jasmine found Jafar in his chamber and demanded that Aladdin be released.

"Sadly, the boy's sentence has been carried out—death," lied Jafar.

Jasmine couldn't believe what Jafar had done. She was heartbroken.

Meanwhile, Aladdin was locked away in the dungeon and could think only of the beautiful princess he would never see again. No matter how much he liked her, she could never love a poor boy like him.

Abu found the cell and unchained Aladdin. Just then, an old prisoner stepped out from the shadows and showed him a way out of the cell.

"There is a cave filled with treasure,"
he whispered. "Treasure enough to
impress your princess."

The old man set Aladdin free in return
for helping him find a special lamp. Aladdin
followed him into the desert. Soon, he and
Abu were standing before the Cave of Wonders!

"Fetch me the lamp, and you
shall have your reward," the old
man promised.
   Aladdin and Abu slowly entered
the cave to search for the lamp.

As Aladdin and Abu entered the cave, they heard a voice: "Touch nothing but the lamp." Soon, they found themselves in a huge cavern filled with coins and jewels.

They met a friendly Magic Carpet who led them to
the magical golden lamp resting on an altar.

Abu had his eye on a very big and sparkly gem. Just as Aladdin reached for the lamp, Abu tried to pick up the large gem. Aladdin tried to stop Abu but it was too late . . . .

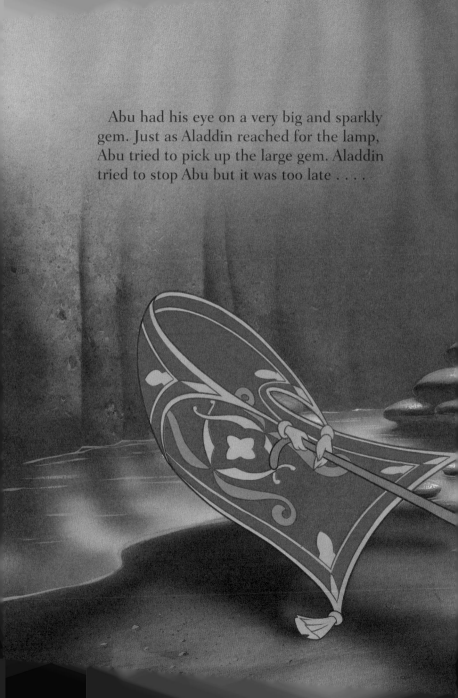

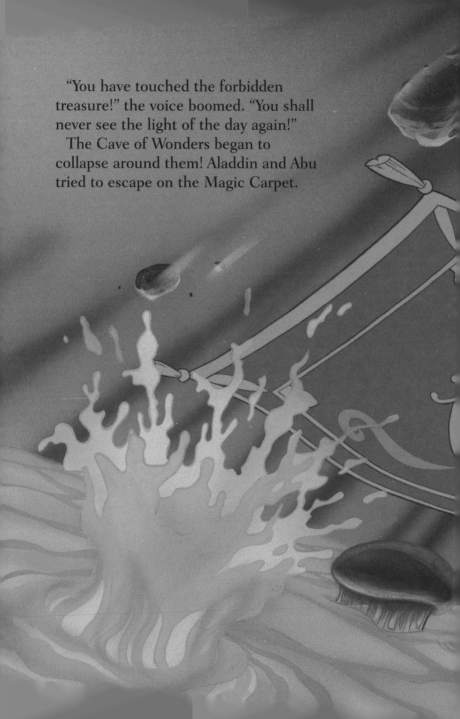

"You have touched the forbidden treasure!" the voice boomed. "You shall never see the light of the day again!"

The Cave of Wonders began to collapse around them! Aladdin and Abu tried to escape on the Magic Carpet.

Before reaching the exit, Aladdin fell off the
Magic Carpet. Frantically, Aladdin grabbed for
a handhold on the crumbling stairs.

The old man waited above. Aladdin begged him
for help.

"Give me the lamp!" the man said, revealing
a dagger.

Abu bit the man's hand. The old man pulled away, and Aladdin and Abu tumbled back into the cave! Luckily, the Magic Carpet stopped their fall, safely setting them on the floor of the cave.

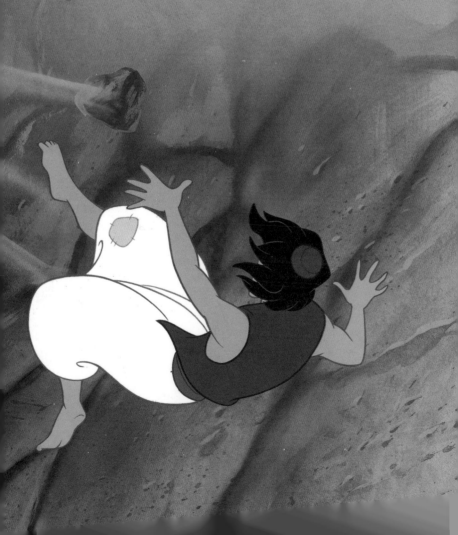

"It's mine!" the old man shrieked, pulling off his
disguise to reveal he was Jafar! As he reached into his
robe for the lamp, he realized it was gone!
"Nooo!" he cried.
Abu had snatched the lamp back from Jafar and
showed it off to Aladdin!

Aladdin looked at the lamp. "I think there's something written here, but it's hard to make out," said Aladdin as he rubbed the lamp. To his astonishment, the lamp began to glow. Then a towering cloud of smoke poured from the spout—and took the form of a giant blue genie!

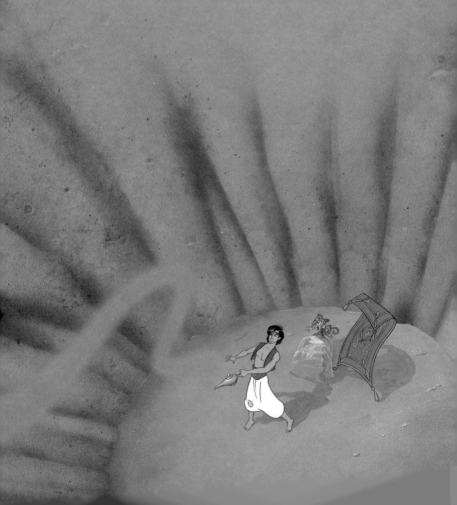

Aladdin couldn't believe he had his own genie. "Are you going to grant me any three wishes I want?" he asked. Aladdin didn't want to waste a wish, so he tricked the Genie.

"Abu, he probably can't even get us out of this cave," Aladdin teased the Genie.

To prove his magical power, the Genie helped them escape.

For his first wish, Aladdin asked, "Can you make me a prince?" Aladdin wanted to impress Princess Jasmine. With a wave of his hands, the Genie dressed Aladdin in clothes fit for a prince!

Later that day, Aladdin arrived at the palace in grand style, introducing himself as Prince Ali Ababwa.

"I have journeyed from afar to seek your daughter's hand in marriage," he announced.

The Sultan was thrilled! But Jasmine thought that he was just another snooty prince.

"I am not a prize to be won!" cried Jasmine, and she ran from the room.

To win Jasmine's heart, Aladdin sneaked up to
her balcony on his Magic Carpet.
    "Princess Jasmine, please give me a chance,"
Aladdin pleaded. "You should be free to make
your own choice." Then he offered her a
Magic Carpet ride.

Together, Aladdin and Jasmine flew through the clouds, over deserts, mountains, and seas, past cities and countrysides, discovering a whole new world.

Jafar was furious to hear that Prince Ali and
Jasmine were growing close. He wanted to marry
Jasmine himself so he could rule Agrabah.
He ordered his guards to chain Prince Ali up—
and throw him into the sea!

"Make sure he is never found," Jafar commanded.

Fortunately, Aladdin had the lamp in his pocket. He summoned the Genie and used his second wish to save himself. Aladdin then raced to the palace on his Magic Carpet.

At the palace, Jafar hypnotized the Sultan again. "Tell Jasmine she must marry me," Jafar ordered.
Suddenly, to Jafar's annoyance, Aladdin entered the room. Aladdin broke the Sultan's staff, revealing Jafar as a traitor. Jafar disappeared before the guards could arrest him.

Later, hiding in his secret chamber, Jafar realized that Prince Ali was just Aladdin and that he had the magical lamp.

The next morning, Iago crept into Aladdin's room and stole the magic lamp. Jafar rubbed the magic lamp, and the Genie appeared.

"I am your master now! I wish to rule . . . as Sultan!"
Jafar ordered.

The Genie was forced to obey. He transformed Jafar into the Sultan. Then, he lifted the palace into the air.

"Genie, no!" Aladdin screamed as Jafar took over the palace.

"Sorry, kid," the Genie said. "I've got a new master now."

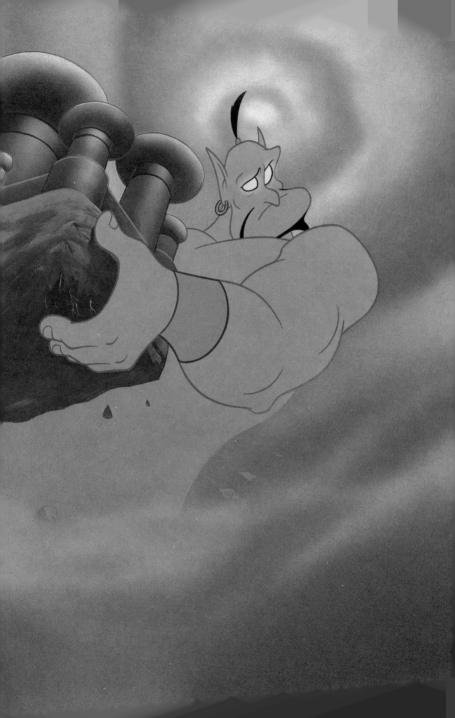

Jafar made his second wish—to become a powerful sorcerer!

Jafar used his evil sorcery to banish Aladdin and Abu to a frozen wasteland. Luckily, the Magic Carpet came to their rescue. "Now, back to Agrabah," Aladdin cried as they sped off on the Magic Carpet.

Back at the palace, the poor Sultan was hanging from the ceiling of his throne room like a puppet. He watched helplessly as Jafar took over his kingdom and made Jasmine his slave.

Jafar was so busy enjoying his power, he almost didn't notice Aladdin sneaking into the throne room. Jasmine tried to distract Jafar, but he saw Aladdin's reflection in her tiara. "How many times do I have to kill you, boy!" roared Jafar.

Aladdin hurled himself
at Jafar. The wicked
sorcerer fired his snake
staff at him and trapped
Aladdin. He even turned
Abu into a toy monkey!

Jasmine ran to help her hero.

"Princess, your time is up!" Jafar said, trapping Jasmine in a huge hourglass!

"You cowardly snake!" shouted Aladdin.

"Snake, am I?" Jafar hissed. The villain turned himself into a gigantic cobra!

Suddenly, Aladdin had an idea that he thought might get rid of Jafar for good.

"The Genie has more power than you'll ever have!" taunted Aladdin. Infuriated, Jafar used his last wish to become an all-powerful genie.

But Jafar forgot that all genies must live in a lamp until they are summoned by a new master. Quickly, Aladdin picked up the lamp and imprisoned Jafar inside it.

"Noooo!" Jafar cried as he was trapped inside the lamp—forever!

Aladdin used his third and final wish to set the Genie free. "No matter what anybody says, you will always be a prince to me," said the grateful Genie to Aladdin.

To Jasmine's delight, the Sultan decided to let the Princess choose her own husband. And there was only one choice!

"I choose you, Aladdin," Jasmine said as she kissed her prince.

And they all lived happily ever after.